THE CONIUM REVIEW
vol. 4

James R. Gapinski
Managing Editor

Amelia Gray
Contest Judge

Chelsea Werner-Jatzke
Editorial Director

Uma Rallabhandi
Senior Editor

Hillary Leftwich
Associate Editor

Holly Tri
Copy Editor

Tristan Beach
Fiction Editor

Justin Carmickle
Fiction Editor

Sarah Colwill-Brown
Fiction Editor

Adam Padgett
Fiction Editor

[contents]

THE CONIUM REVIEW

vol. 4

Conium Press
Portland, OR

The Conium Review
Vol. 4
© 2015 Conium Press
Portland, OR

http://www.coniumreview.com

ISBN-10 1942387032
ISBN-13 978-1-942387-03-9
ISSN 2164-6252

Library of Congress Control Number: 2015956673

Cover Image: © qiujusong / Dollar Photo Club
Internal Images: © qiujusong / Dollar Photo Club
Layout & Design: James R. Gapinski and Uma Rallabhandi

[contents]

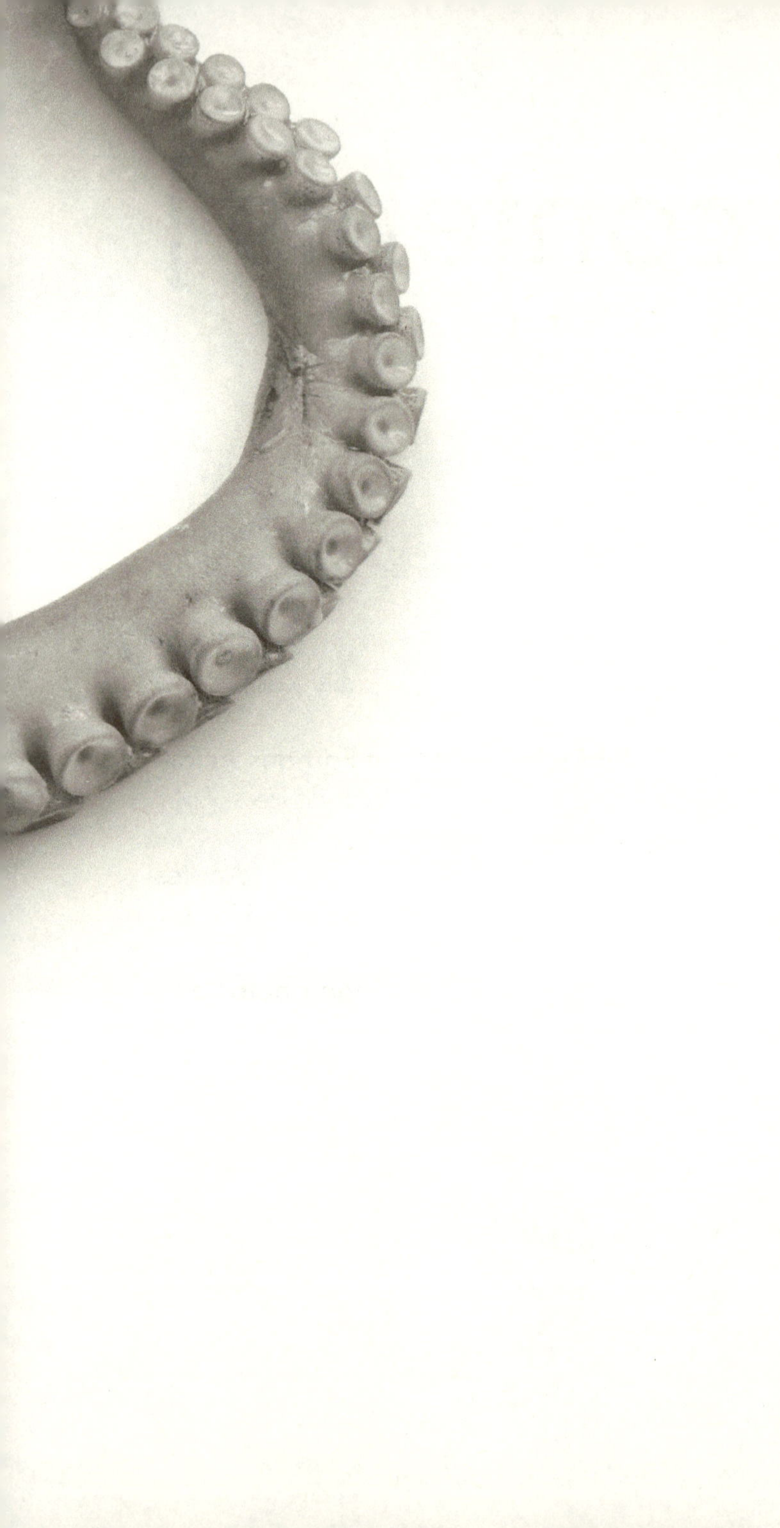

THE PEOPLE WHO LIVE IN THE SEARS

INNOVATIVE SHORT FICTION CONTEST WINNER

Emily Koon

THE PEOPLE WHO LIVE IN THE SEARS

Emily Koon

The people who lived in the Sears didn't want to leave. The store's management worried about their bulging red eyes, the way they stalked customers browsing for camouflage pants and adult onesies. Sales were down, which meant the Sears was in danger of closing, which meant the mall would soon have a hole in its south wing. Downhill from there.

Until now, the people in the Sears were tolerated as long as they stayed out of the way. *Don't harass the shoppers, don't use the gas ranges. And no sex anywhere on Consolidated Capital Partners property,* not that this mattered. The people who lived in the Sears weren't interested in sex. They were interested in peace, in continuity, and now they were being pushed out.

"To optimize the browsing experience of our guests," the written notice said. Everyone knew this was about the guy who watched the Food Network in his underpants.

The people stared at the store manager with their red bug eyes and told him what they thought. Life was easy in the Sears. Every morning, they could waddle down to Starbuck's and slurp triple espresso macchiatos until their hearts gave out. No boss on the horn, no hassles.

If he thought they'd give that up without a fight, he was tripping.

"Can you guys just get out of here?" the manager said. "The semi-annual sale is coming up, and you losers can't be weirding out the customers."

He'd thought of living in the Sears once too, but outside never got bad enough. Last month he got the director's cut DVDs of *Battlestar Galactica* and marathoned them with the okay-looking Kirkland's cashier. They made out a little, and it was better than nothing. He thought while kissing her, *This wouldn't be happening if I was living in the Sears.*

The manager was a punk, little more than a kid. The older residents could bully him, but what if they sent in the big guns? The lawyers, the mall cops packing pepper spray. The only things the people in the Sears had for weapons were barbecue tongs. If it came to that, what good were barbecue tongs against a law enforcement infrastructure? Not much.

The people who lived in the Sears formed a big circle around the escalator, hands across America, and realized they had something more powerful than barbecue tongs. They held hands and felt like one giant heart beating together, thrump thrump thrump. Loud enough to drown out Celine Dion, the misbehaving children, the beauty counter ladies baiting customers, the back-to-schoolers trying on Keds. They thrumped so loud they thought they could silence the whole world.

•   •   •

Some of the people in the Sears had been there since the '80s, when the mall was built. They got used to the pillow-top mattresses and sectional sofas, the suede espadrilles that made their calves look good, and stayed. The newbies were living out their teenage fantasy of getting locked in the mall overnight. In that fantasy, they tried on all the clothes and fancy dresses they wanted, and what was a fancy dress without a makeover at the Estee Lauder counter? Nothing, that's what. Happiness came after they jumped the display cases and caked foundation on themselves, after they spritzed on Malibu Musk and passed out from the godawful pleasure. Now they could do this every day.

There were dozens, maybe hundreds of people living in the Sears. A few more trickled in every week as they fled failed marriages and the abysmal job market. After the economic upswing, they fled the job opportunities, the compulsion to work. The veterans napped all day. The newbies fretted, not yet lost in the readymade comforts.

"What do you do about food? What's the policy on toilets? Where do you shower?" were the first questions newbies asked, always in that order. Eat, poop, wash.

One of the veterans would pull the newbie out of Small Appliances or Fine China, wherever they were when they realized, *This is it, I live in the Sears now, the mall is my town*. Then the freakout over logistics. They'd pat the newcomer's arms and give them the rundown, how easy everything would be now, the blissful few choices left to make.

"The food court is open from nine to nine, ten on weekends. The demo Jacuzzi is communal. Shit where you can."

When the veterans first came, they didn't have guides. They had to figure things out for themselves. It was pretty lonely, circling the store all day, pretending to shop. At night they'd climb into the display beds and think about the lives they'd left. Should they go back? Patch things up with Susan? All these years later, they wondered. Who had Susan been? What had she meant to them? There was a vague memory of a drive-in movie theater and Coca-Cola spilled in their laps. *E.T. the Extra-Terrestrial.* Wonder if that's still playing.

■ ■ ■

Back to School season was a tense time for everybody. The friction between the shoppers and the people who lived in the Sears had a smell, like burning rubber.

"Put that *Pirates of the Caribbean* backpack right back where you found it, asshole," said the people who lived in the Sears.

The shoppers complained to the manager, or they didn't buy the backpack, Reebok sneakers, patterned tights. Worst case, a stressed-out parent took on the person who lived in the Sears and stood their ground. There were a scary couple of seconds where everybody thought the person who lived in the Sears would lose their shit. Once in a while, they did.

An urban legend dating back to the 1990s said a mother and her teenage daughter were imprisoned for two days in a camping tent, having bought the last pair of acid wash jeans with shredded knees. The people who lived in the Sears had just kind of snapped. No one was espousing force, but they could all see the people who were living in the Sears then had felt oppressed, like wild animals losing their habitat.

"We do not come into your house and take things out of your closet!" the protest signs read that year. The signs this year read, "A Return to Sanity." It was right there on the signs, what the movement was about. They just wanted to send a message—ours, yours. No one meant to burn down the mall.

. . .

The fire started the way all fires start, with a gas camping stove.

Sporting Goods went up like a tinderbox. The explosion blew the revolution's leader backwards into the portrait studio, and when the paramedics pulled her out, her eyebrows and most of her hair were gone. The people who'd lived in the Sears blinked at her in the bright sunlight, which some of them hadn't seen in years. Disoriented, disappointed, they slinked off. She was this injured pink thing no one could see leading a revolt.

Inside the store, the fire raged like it had been waiting for someone to set it. As if it had been carried around inside each of the people who lived in the Sears until the match was lit near that camp stove's leaking gas valve. The people who lived in the Sears weren't trying to burn the place down, the fire knew this. They were trying to light a small flame, buy the world a Coke, in hopes the people who lived outside the Sears would become sensitive to their plight. But once the fire was out, it raged.

"I'm a fire, man, that's what we do," it said as it gutted the Lancôme counter.

After the cosmetics counters, the fire took out Juniors with its display of Justin Bieber t-shirts, then Bed and Bath. All that was left was a set of NASA-grade, flame-retardant Wamsutta comforters. At the end of the world, the fire thought, when it was done raging, there would be nothing left but cockroaches and Wamsutta comforters.

After the fire was done with the Sears, it took the rest of the mall. The Kirkland's, the Barnes & Noble, the orthopedic shoe place, each abandoned by its staff and rubbled. The fire's only regret was for the beautiful charred things left in its wake.

"Man, that scrolled wine holder would have looked great in the kitchen."

Then it remembered it was fire. It kept going.

.   .   .

The fire moved on to the surrounding commercial district, swallowing the Chili's and the wireless phone carrier. The people who worked in these businesses had watched the mall burn, thinking of Mt. Saint Helens erupting on television when they were children. The black and gray smoke was as they remembered. So were their thoughts that somehow this was connected to the end of the world, that all the malls in the country were bursting into flames, just as they'd thought all the volcanoes in the world were erupting.

The mall was built when they were kids, around the same time Mt. Saint Helens blew its top. Before that, the whole area was open farmland with a dairy. Once, the school took them on a field trip to the dairy. The farmer let them drink fresh cream and pet baby goats wearing crocheted sweaters. They hadn't thought about the goats in years.

.   .   .

Because the people who'd lived in the Sears didn't have

anywhere else to go, they walked east toward the national forest. They couldn't recall much about their old lives, but they thought there'd once been a city on the other side of the forest. If they were remembering right, there was a Sears in it. The city had a skyscraper with a restaurant at the top that slowly turned all day. When your drinks came, you might be looking at the skyline; when your dessert came, you'd be looking at trees.

The fire was ahead of them, but when they turned southeast, taking to the highway, it raged alongside them in the distance. If they turned their heads just right, they didn't have to look at it. Eventually, the fire was only visible as gray smoke above the national forest.

"Who would set a forest on fire?" one of them asked.

An old-timer shook his head. The others worried he wasn't strong enough to make it to the new Sears. "Damn shame, if you ask me," he said. He remembered going to the forest when his children were small. It had trails and swing sets that his pigtailed daughter liked to swing on. "All those memories up in smoke."

"How does a thing like that happen?" the others wanted to know.

It didn't take them long to forget. The moment the road forked and they found the fire could be put out of sight, their thoughts returned to their lives in the Sears. The old-timer was thinking further back than that, to his daughter on the swings again. She'd worn fat bows of orange yarn on each of her pigtails. He couldn't remember what became of her.

．　．　．

After the fire ravaged the first suburb, it moved on to the

rabbit warren of cheap pueblo-style deathtraps in the second. The residents saw the mall fire on television and ignored the warning to evacuate, insisting that suburbs were a zone free of sorrow. This was why they'd moved out here in the first place. Life in the city was suffocating. Other people's dramas played out at the community level—neighbors fighting, passed out drunk in the hallways. The women were followed off the subways by men who pretended to live in the buildings and then tried to force their way into the apartments. As soon as they had the money saved, they bought these places.

The news said the blaze started in the Sears. The woman who lived in the cul-de-sac unit thought of her sister, who'd been a real firecracker, going out on her own to start an insurance business. They lost touch after it failed. She heard the sister was living in a Sears somewhere, that people did this, that Sears was maybe not a store at all but an assisted living facility for the maladjusted. Or it was a store once, but people took it over.

A handful of people made it out of the suburb. The cul-de-sac woman threw whatever she could grab into a Jazzercise bag, leaving the rubber exercise bands that were already in there for managing stress on the road. She added protein bars and her signed photo of Ed McMahon. She never did win the Publishers Clearing House Sweepstakes, probably wouldn't now that the world was ending and Ed McMahon was dead. Had he died in the flames, or had he been gone for years already? She couldn't remember.

By the time the survivors from the suburb set out, it was hard to tell the places in the town that were on fire from the places that weren't. They saw that the fire had always been raging around them, that they were a part of it. Each of them a single flame lick capable of destroying everything.

. . .

On the third day, the group that had left the Sears approached the valley where the new Sears was rumored to be. Down in the valley, which earlier that day contained their hopes, was an entire town on fire. Its mall was already a smoking crater, along with the Walmart and Church's Chicken and concentric circles of craftsman houses. The skyscraper with the rotating restaurant was still standing, but one side of it was being eaten away by the fire, which hated to destroy a unique piece of architecture like that. From their cliff, the people who'd lived in the Sears could see the fire extended to the horizon in every direction. They couldn't go around it.

"Perhaps we've made a wrong turn somewhere," they said. "This can't be it. It's on fire."

"This has to be it. This is where the Sears *is*," one of them said. She emphasized *is* because Sears *was*, and nothing, not a fire or the end of the world or corporate bankruptcy, could change what was an undeniable fact of being.

By now their pack had grown. People escaping the burning suburbs on foot folded into their ranks. The families, the woman who kept taking exercise bands out to perform fly presses. The man who wouldn't stop talking about goats in sweaters, who was certain this same fire was happening everywhere, in every town in America, maybe the world.

They headed back up the cliff, a gang of hundreds, thousands, slowed by the old-timer, who they'd hoped to lose by now. The group was so big, so slow, so mad at the old-timer that at first they didn't notice the flames licking up the hill behind them. When they finally smelled the burned flesh of the stragglers, including (thank God), the old-timer, the ones who were able to ran—up the cliff, back to the highway, toward any town that wasn't burning, toward whatever Sears in whatever part of the country was still left standing to welcome them.

CAMISOLE

Tamara K. Walker

CAMISOLE

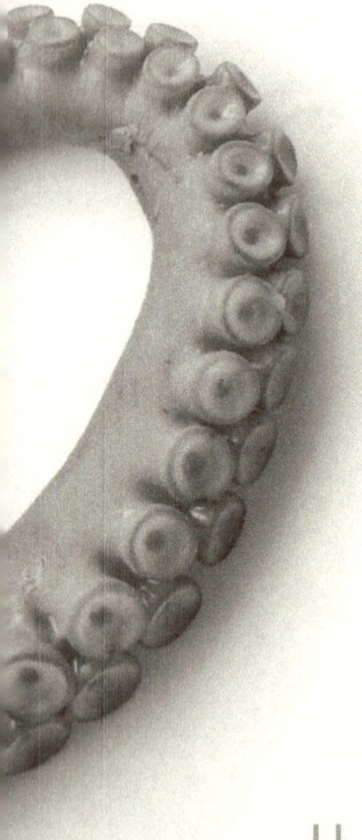

Tamara K. Walker

The first time was at the shooting range, and I really am sorry about that. I bought one of those compact pink handguns marketed to women and set about immediately learning how to use it responsibly. I exist out of society, smiling deities, and every jurisdiction, so I must ensure my own protection. I regretted it immediately. Firearms. What a funny term. Arms. Whatever I may have felt in my whole time of using the thing, I've never once felt even remotely that it was an extension of my arm. It always felt foreign. A remote control for holes. A remote hole control.

I was practicing surgically placing those holes in paper targets, you by my side, when inexplicably, I slipped and it went off, barrel point-blank at your neck. You were wearing that light peach camisole, the one with the built-in shelf bra. You smiled sideways wryly and said that it was okay this one time. A pinpoint formed on the exact same spot on my neck that later grew into a mole. We went for lunch and you ordered three salads.

I saw that same cami by itself in a dryer at the laundromat and you were nowhere to be found. It was then that I considered doing it there, in the putrid, hyperreal mix of florescence and daylight, on the dank tile in front of everyone, squeeze-don't-jerk, bang bang bang. Maybe when you came in a week or whenever to pick up your cami. But then I rethought it: no, that was just a shade too cliché; it's probably happened before, and even if not, the laundromat is the kind of place that not-so-subtly invites these things. Impersonal, always tense, and of course, the lighting.

The second time was not an accident. You *were* reaching for the remote that day; we were going to play something or watch something, wearing little. You leaned forward and everything was gray, including the cami I was wearing, which was white. I squeezed one shot into your brain stem and two into your right hip, flared out the way you were sitting. You looked confused. You were fine. Two holes in my hip oozed vanishing cartoon blood and then breathed weird evaporating voids, cool as if you had licked them under a fan. We continued watching Netflix and inhaled vegetable fried rice. I didn't notice the one at the base of my skull until I got home and found my hair matted with something wet that had dried.

Neither was the third. Yarn shop. Your shift. Forehead. Blink bam. Same thing. Had to cover my forehead with a badly knitted teal beret.

No, the holes always appearing in my body after shooting you are not symbols. This is not a didactic tale. The places where I aimed are not symbolic, and neither is the gun itself a symbol. Calm down. I'm trying to tell you what happened. Call quality is dreadful these days.

I saw you at the library earlier this week, and I could have done it then. It was so tempting as you passed me in the sci-fi aisle, adult fiction section, conspicuously pushing your round-owl wire frames up the bridge of your nose and sneering like a high school frenemy. But the library is the opposite of the laundromat and that wouldn't do either. They have a security guard and it's too quiet. You exited, taunting me, looking over your shoulder and pointing to the faint X you drew in pencil on the back of your beige cami. Dos and don'ts. Daring me is a don't. Doesn't work.

The bank. Smells like leather and pencils. I didn't even think about it; meaning, of course, I started to. But you don't mess with the bank. It's deadly serious and would apparently be over the line. Law enforcement is unpleasant to deal with when friendly; I really don't want to see them hostile. Not the bank; just like I can't shoot myself and have you wear the remote-controlled holes, since this is a one-way street. How unfair. You can only turn right on red from a one-way street onto a one-way street, just like I can't turn a metaphor. Moving on.

I approached you at your potter's wheel, back turned, looking completely oblivious, which made me uneasy that you might not have been. I'd been hunting you for quite a while. At least since the third time. Or the library. Like I said, I have to ensure my own protection.

I had to get you when you were creating. You would have wanted me to shoot a ceramic pot on the wall in front of you and have it explode dramatically into sharp fragments. You: coffee-colored camisole, hair up in a ponytail, good posture. I put some xylitol gum under my tongue, wanting the artificially sweetened flavor fresh, walked briskly forward, unfocused my eyes, and fired one, two, three staccato shots into your basal ganglia. Startled, your hand sunk into the side of the soft urn you were working on, and I saw the clay rotate rapidly around it, entrenching the malformation. Ouch. How satisfying. I gasped as three holes dilated into existence on the right side of my chest opposite my heart. Like indigo dye packs going off. Like I had just shoplifted something. My white cami. High-frequency sound and deleted air rushed through them.

I saw the cami I was wearing that day spinning alone at the bottom of my tiny washing machine, the one that clothes never shrink in but that always shrinks itself with every load. Anyway, I think it's had too many washes. It's getting grayish, and I can barely even tell that it's white. Oh, yes, that mole. Let's do an inventory. I thought it might be cancerous, so I went to a dermatologist. It's benign, but I had it removed for aesthetic reasons. There's a faint X mark where it was. I only regret kind of lying to you about the symbols.

PASSING

Rita Bullwinkel

PASSING

Rita Bullwinkel

I have twenty-four haircuts worth of grief, twenty-four times since the barber has taken her razor to my nape, eight years, three trims a year, since my husband was taken from me, dragged out into the night and transported by bus or train or foot (I don't even know) to the tundra, some land covered with snow, and if not snow, then barren prairie, where not even the birds know how to survive. My barber cuts the front parts first and then works her way to the rear.

I go in to get a haircut. I see my gray hair fall in snips; clumps of white are strewn across the barber's floor. I see my husband, an inch tall, shoveling the white away, clearing the walkway to his barrack, pushing my wisps of hair aside, out of the way; watch out, I tell him, watch out, another one is falling, another piece of hair coming your way, it's a big one, better move before it falls.

I keep my hair short in a bob with straight bangs that hit just above the eyebrow. It's the same cut I had when my husband went away. But my hair, back then, was black and, of course, now it's gray. Perhaps my gray is a gift from my husband, something stealthily sent to me, some piece of his world, the white snow, that he wants to share with me, and this was the only way he knew how.

I save the hair in jars to document the time passing. Each cut gets its own jar. I built a shelf to house them. The jars spectrum from dark to light, from night to white, from black to the absence of color. The gray-haired jars are kinked so the hair looks larger, like more was cut, but it is just the added volume of the wave. Six, twelve, eighteen, twenty-four, I think those are the appropriate deviations. Those are the years that make sense to group together. Those are the time periods that are easiest for me to see.

I fantasize about emptying the jars on my bed and mixing together all of the colors, making a salt and pepper soup and stuffing all the hair into one grand vessel sealed at the top center. My life in haircuts, my husband's absence in snips, my shelf bowing with the wait of glass jars whose contents are waiting to be combined.

When I see my husband in visions, his hair is long, all the way down to his knees, and his beard erupts from his face, grown past his shoulders and down to his belly, where it matts at the ends. He smiles and his grand beard smiles with him. No time has passed for him. He has no cuts by which to mark the rotations of the sun. His hair will grow long enough till the wardens can fashion it into a noose and then they'll hang him by his own hair on a rafter.

I have asked the camp to send me my husband's hair after they are done with him. I will cut the noose up into individual strands and mix it with my own trimmings and light the pile on fire so our hair burns together in a deep hole I have dug in our backyard in the ground.

DICTATOR IN A JAR

Marina Petrova

DICTATOR IN A JAR

Marina Petrova

After Todd left, my apartment filled with water. When I come home from work, I dive in through the front door and swim up and down between the couch and the refrigerator. It's quieter underwater. Two Todd-less months have passed. But I haven't fallen apart, not at all. I've been setting alarms, taking showers, overcooking eggs, going to the office, flossing my teeth before bed, keeping up with the routine that earns me the right to answer *fine* when someone asks how I am doing. I renewed my Netflix subscription. I'm holding it together, aquatically speaking. It's not like I've been shedding pieces, leaving bone chips, muscle threads, and slivers of skin all over the plain, like a house spread over a prairie by a tornado.

"What happened here?" a plainclothes detective would ask a uniformed policeman, ducking under the yellow tape across my front door.

"She fell apart after her boyfriend dumped her," the policeman would reply, lifting one of my kidneys from on top of the reading lamp and dropping it into the evidence bag. "That's our working theory."

"So the death appears to be accidental?"

It's not like that.

It's like Todd, the dumper, is riding into the sunset on a horse by the name of Black Valor, wearing a bowler hat. He would wear a bowler hat or name his horse that. Meanwhile, I am at work, floating in phone silence and unwanted sympathy. Beverly, our office manager, has been stroking my arm.

"You look good, honey. Have you lost weight?"

More than company, misery loves a spectator. I would die on my kitchen floor, alone, with a broken hip, unable to reach the phone after slipping in a puddle of tasteless fat-free yogurt. No one would hear my anonymous whimpers. The cats would feast on my internal organs and the neighbors, after days of enthusiastic meowing, would call the authorities. The cats would have to be dragged away. Beverly would wear a tasteful, black A-line dress to my funeral and lament predictable blunders of the Fortuna.

Not so fast, Beverly, I should have said. I had a plan—I would buy a Life Alert button.

Also, I don't have cats. If I were ever to get cats, I would invest in an automatic feeder, so they would last a couple of weeks before eating my dead corpse.

What I told Beverly was *thank you* and left the office.

I walked home mumbling, practicing snarky remarks I would make tomorrow. It was chilly. Trees brushed their red and yellow highlights off their foreheads and all restaurants, coffee shops, and nail salons wore October in chestnut suede. A new store had opened in place of my favorite Vietnamese restaurant, the one that closed for health violations a month after Todd left. Construction crews were gone and there was a black and yellow banner with a smiley face:

Disposable Keepsakes
Grand Opening

I decided to check it out. Todd used to say that I never did anything spontaneous.

The space inside was no more than twenty square feet and smelled like a rainy Sunday afternoon nap. There were rows and rows of shelves stacked with cardboard boxes, glass jars, small feathered birds on wooden platforms, looking disturbingly real, toasters, wind chimes, dried flowers, beach postcards, things you would never buy in your own hometown. The clerk at the counter had pierced cheeks and a lush black beard rolled up like a rollercoaster. He yawned.

"How can I help you?"

"What's in the boxes?" I asked.

"Things you don't know you need until you have them."

That sounded right. I didn't know I needed Todd until one day I found him aerodynamically attached to my couch and to my Seamless account. I picked up a box the size of a milk carton, mostly to distract myself, to keep from crying in front of the pompous bearded guy.

"That's a good one," he reassured me.

"What is it?"

"It's a miniature dictator. Read the label: *Dictator in a Jar*."

"What does it do?"

"It lives in a jar, that's all. It grows in less than twenty-four hours."

"How much?"

"Twenty-six dollars and ninety-five cents, plus tax. There are instructions included inside."

Sometimes, when nothing else makes sense, all you

want to hear is that instructions are included.

My apartment woke up when I turned the lights on. The couch stretches and meows like a cat I do not have when I come home. The umbrella stand, the bookcase, and the vase on the coffee table stir. One has to live alone to notice these things. I threw the remnants of yesterday's sandwich into the trash and opened the dictator box. Inside, there were two clear packets with powder (one white, one blue) and a plastic spoon. There was also a two-page instructions sheet.

Grow a Dictator — Instructions:
1. *Pour contents of Bag 1 into a large glass jar (jar not included).*
2. *Add 2 cups of warm water, mix until smooth.*
3. *Rinse spoon well.*
4. *Slowly stir in contents of Bag 2. Warning: substance in Bag 2 is harmful if inhaled or swallowed.*
5. *Stir for additional 10 minutes or until the mixture reaches consistency of clotted cream.*
6. *Place the jar under direct sunlight. If sunlight is not available, place under a table lamp. Warning: without natural light the dictator may not grow above 2 inches in height.*

I had a jar of pickles in my fridge or, rather, a jar of pickle. All of its companions had perished in a Civil War documentary marathon I had watched in my maniacally insomniac state. *Sorry about this,* I said to the last pickle, watching it go down the toilet with its bathwater, *but this happens to the best of us.* I washed the jar twice, but it still smelled of pickle juice. I followed the instructions, being super careful not to swallow or inhale the contents of Bag 2. What would happen if I did?

"It appears to be an overdose," a uniformed officer would say to a plainclothes detective. "Drugs," he would add, "again," shaking his head dejectedly.

"Don't jump to conclusions," the detective would reply. "There is pickle juice under her fingernails and the liquefaction of all the internal organs might be a sign of foul play."

I placed the jar on the kitchen windowsill (with the southern exposure, my dictator should grow nicely) and called my father. The kitchen sink was leaking again, and Deborah, his neighbor's wife, had moved out again, he said. She would tell her husband that she couldn't live like this each year around Halloween. By Christmas, she would figure out that *this* was not that bad and come back. I would send a check and visit in a couple of weeks, I said. I watched the phone go dark on my nightstand. Someone might text. Todd wouldn't text. I wouldn't want him to. If he did, I would tell him to eat Black Valor's shit.

Falling asleep used to be a way of slipping into the future. Todd and I are in the car, stuck in traffic after a day of playing volleyball and swimming in the ocean. The windows are open, I have beach hair, and Todd's hand is on my lap. Or we are hiking upstate, maybe even apple picking. It's a warm and sincere day, painted with oil colors that stay inside the lines. Little innocuous scenes, nothing grandiose, not walking down the aisle or choosing adjacent cemetery plots. I still see these scenes but now, but instead of Todd and me, it's Todd and Sasha.

Sasha is wearing two types of stripes, horizontal and vertical, and she is pulling it off. Meanwhile, someone is taking a hot iron to my stomach lining.

In the morning there was a clump on top of the clotted cream, covered with tiny sharp teeth and spikey grey hair. I poked it with a fork and it jiggled. Gross. I would have thrown it out immediately, but my building has a strict recycling policy. I told the clump that I would deal with it after work. I'm late for a meeting, I said. It was a bagel Friday at the office.

I work for a company that facilitates communication between other companies that, best I can tell, are having difficulties communicating. I enter numbers into a spreadsheet and compare them to the numbers I entered a year ago. If the percent change turns red, indicating a negative, I send an email to my boss with the spreadsheet attached and a red exclamation point for *Important* in the subject line, informing him that he should be alarmed because communication is not going well. Why these companies are having difficulties communicating, I cannot say. Maybe, at times, asking for what you want is too daunting. Other times, when you ask, it doesn't work out.

I don't think about Todd at work. I think about numbers, font sizes, and choices. What's for lunch? How do I pick the cleanest bathroom stall? Why does my boss's forehead sweat like a block of cheese taken out of the refrigerator? I read bullet-pointed lists with instructions on how to be happy. I think about avoiding Beverly and about manatees. Todd and I once argued for hours about whether a manatee could fit into a bathtub. Mostly, I think about Todd. I anticipate the flood of dumb silence at home.

But around six o'clock, on this average bagel Friday, I walked into my kitchen and dropped the mail on the floor, stupefied. A little figure, no more than four inches tall, wearing avocado-colored trousers and jacket, square-toed leather boots, and gun holsters under both arms, was pacing inside my pickle-less jar, hands clasped behind his back. He saw me, paused with one foot in the air, and began to feverishly scratch his round, puffy cheeks.

I remembered Benny, the hamster I had when I was seven. Benny also had puffy cheeks, which grew rounder when he stuffed them with grain. Except for the one time when Benny didn't get to stuff his cheeks, because our family took a weeklong vacation to Myrtle Beach and I forgot to leave him food. My father refused to show me what Benny's cheeks looked like upon our return.

"Where have you been all day?"

Three red exclamation points—*it* could talk. Benny couldn't; that may have been his downfall. I would have listened to a small creature with a deep voice, furry or human.

"The facial hair fiasco must be addressed immediately! Batting your eyelashes won't do." He stopped scratching for a second then resumed with a renewed intensity. "Look at my face. There's nothing! No pointy beard, no mustache, no goatee, not even a five o'clock shadow. Are you some kind of an amateur who cannot follow simple instructions?"

He was insinuating that I was a failure, a person who couldn't assemble an IKEA bed or who missed airplanes, lost driver's licenses, or fell into crocodile pits with clear warning signs. *Falling Into Crocodile Pit Will Cause Immediate Dismemberment!*

He pressed his small but menacing face against the glass.

"I'm asking you a question! When I ask, you answer, unless I command you not to. Then I would say 'silence!' Did I say 'silence'? That is not a rhetorical question. I don't ask rhetorical questions; this isn't some slow-progressing, incurable disease support group. Where is my facial hair?"

"Maybe it will still grow?" My voice came out rickety.

"Maybe? Maybe a unicorn will win in a church bingo game and buy you half of a brain. Maybe a man in a clown suit will smuggle some sense into you through the airport security checkpoint in a tube of toothpaste. Maybe the next time you will rinse the spoon better. Can't you read? Are you crying? Why are you crying?"

Why would I be crying? It was not like a miniature dictator in a pickle jar was berating me. Not like every day a manatee died in a collision with a propeller-driven boat. Not like I had no clue that Todd was breaking up with me until after it had happened. It was nothing like that. *You're not going to cry*, Todd had said.

"I'm hungry," the dictator said.

"I have cheese."

Benny had eaten grain. Do dictators eat cheese?

"Coffee beans!" he yelled. "Do I look like a rat to you? Were you dropped on your head as a baby or is critical thinking not a part of your daily routine? Come on, don't cry."

No wonder he was agitated; caffeine is an addiction.

I poured coffee beans into the jar. The dictator shaped

them into a pyramid, broke a bean in two, and chewed each half with the vigor of a man who had been lost in the woods for days. He made slurping noises and picked his teeth with his middle finger. He looked at me, appeased.

"Better," he said. He sniffed the air inside the jar. "What's that smell? It smells like a sour dishrag died in here."

I must have given him a look. He changed the subject.

"I have three modes: *march on*, *think big*, and *dictate*. By default, I am always in the *march on* mode, but if you clap twice, I will switch to *think big*."

I clapped twice. I'm a people pleaser.

He sat down cross-legged, furrowed his thick brows, and propped his chin with his fists. He had a jawline of a baby seal, which explained the need for the beard. He chewed his thumbnail and spit into clotted cream, drawing air loudly through his nostrils.

I had to ask. "What are you thinking about?"

"Who told you that you could interrupt? My thoughts will be disclosed on a need to know basis. If you need to know, I was thinking about what I always think about—world domination and unicycles."

"Why do you think about unicycles?"

"Because riding one requires incredible poise and equilibrium. I have a dexterous mind, which allows me to think outside the box. You could learn a thing or two about that. You didn't bother asking why I thought about world domination."

"You're the thing in a jar," I said.

Todd used to complain about my neighbor's two yappy Maltese leaving puddles by the mailboxes. Couldn't she walk them on time? *She is old*, I said, *she has arthritis. Then she shouldn't keep dogs*, he said. *People have done worse not to be alone*, I said. That's when Todd told me I was thinking inside the box.

"Mutiny will be reprimanded," the dictator said and ate another coffee bean. "I'm the authority here, the malevolent despot, if you'd like." He stomped a miniature boot and splashed the lapels of his jacket and his nose with clotted cream. "I give orders. I dictate and you take notes. Clap three times."

I clapped. The dictator got up, cracked his knuckles, and began to pace again, nodding with each step.

"Write this down," he said, "word for word."

I brought a spiral notebook and a pen from the bedroom—tomorrow, when Beverly asks me what I did last night, I would say *not much*, with the satisfaction of knowing it to be not true. The dictator cleared his throat:

"Our empirical knowledge of marine life forms is limited. Acantharian is a type of large amoeba that lives in open waters. In this case, large is a relative term. This microscopic animal has a skeleton made of a single sulfate crystal cell. It quickly dissolves into the ocean water after the cell dies. Together with other microscopic organisms, these amoebas account for most of the biomass on Earth."

What would happen if I dissolved?

"The landlord hasn't seen her for over a month," a uniformed policeman would say, breaking the lock on my front door. "He is concerned. The place is rent-stabilized."

"She dissolved," the detective would reply. "It's a normal process. Call the next of kin." Maybe the detective would be an amoeba as well.

That night I slept and no one took a hot iron to my stomach.

We've fallen into a routine, the dictator and I. It worried me a little. Todd, about a month before he had left, showed me a black and white photograph he had taken in my stairwell—a crumpled milk carton leaning against an empty champagne bottle. He said it represented monotony and looked at me as if I didn't understand metaphors. Maybe, I told him, it represented unrealistic expectations.

The dictator expects coffee beans each morning. He also expects that I put him in the *dictate* mode at least once a night and diligently take notes. He knows a lot about marine animals. I asked him to tell me about manatees, but he said that I don't get to dictate what he dictates. I ate cheese quesadillas for lunch yesterday. Beverly has stopped complimenting me on my weight loss.

He is a bit bossy. Things he doesn't like include, but are not limited to, my being late from work, cheap coffee beans, reality television, electronic music (he loves classical, though, especially Brahms), bright colors (I wore a neon green t-shirt the other day; what sort of pathetic cry for attention is this, he asked; he can be insensitive at times), small dogs, and sunny weather. The latter, he says, makes people step out of line. Suffice it to say that he doesn't like that. On weekdays, when I leave for work, he demands to know when I will be home. He thinks my job is silly.

"What could you be doing there for nine hours?"

I tried to explain. "Companies," I said, "have trouble communicating. We have a software system that tracks the efficiency of responses and sometimes crashes. These efficiencies fluctuate, go up and down, but it's hard to tell which is which because people use words and assume they are being understood. In business, that's called optimism. That's why we compare trends to a year ago."

"That's because you live in a developed country and there is nothing here to do," the dictator said. "You could be laying railroads through tundra or building power transmission lines in rural areas."

I threatened to put a lid on the jar and tighten it. He accused me of mutiny again, but his lower lip quivered. I should've told him that I don't suffocate those who become dependent on me. That's more of a Todd thing.

The day Todd dumped me the weather was harmless—partly cloudy. I texted him a joke about two raccoons and a pogo stick. He replied: *Ha.* One Ha, no exclamation point, no smiley face, no winky face, not even a second Ha. That should have been an indication of communication not going well. Around four in the afternoon, he texted me: *meet at Café Fortuna.* When I got there, at seven as we had agreed, he was already sitting at the table with a beer and that face, a nervous face, the one your underwear would make if your pants unexpectedly fell off.

"Listen," he said, "sometimes in this vast sea of people you meet one person who is not like other people."

Yes, I thought, I knew.

"This world is filled with amazing people, floor to ceiling, but you buy bananas, right?"

I nodded. I liked bananas.

"You buy them in a bunch. They could all be superb bananas: ripe, not mushy, no difference in sweetness or smoothness of taste. But in the whole bunch, there is usually one banana with that little blue sticker. It might be random, you know, some dudester put a sticker on this banana without giving it much thought. Why this one? Still, there is one banana with a sticker and the rest without. You can't dispute that."

I didn't, though the word *dudester* irritated my eardrum. I thought I was the banana with a sticker. That was nice. Maybe he was about to ask if we could move in together; although, for all practical purposes, he was already pretty much moved into my place and my socks had even vacated their dresser drawer to make room for his camera equipment.

"I think," Todd said ordering a second beer, "you're a great banana. I don't want to hurt your feelings. It's not that Sasha is superior to you, objectively speaking; it's that, for me, she has that blue sticker. This was unavoidable, like a freight train speeding out of control down a steep hill, with an operator that has fallen asleep."

Oh, but that train was clearly avoidable. All Todd had to do to avoid that train was not to step on the damned tracks. He said Sasha was unconventional. She was not bound to a routine—she had a fashion blog. She also sold secondhand designer handbags on eBay and small quantities of pot out of her apartment, which was how Todd had met her.

"This is the time in our lives to experience the experiences that will define who we are when we are old. You're not going to cry, are you?"

I didn't. I made it back to my apartment without crying. Technically, not the entire way, but the elevator doesn't count. No one was watching. Maybe the doorman was watching through his little camera, but he might not have known what I was doing. And people have done worse things in elevators. Todd once told me in an elevator that my teeth looked big.

The dictator was now drawing hearts in the clotted cream with his index finger. They had zigzag fractures and were pierced by feathered arrows.

"Think about it," he said, "railroads are hardly ever misunderstood. If you need to build a railroad, you take a blueprint of a railroad, you know it is one, and you build it. You don't accidentally build a carousel. We should travel north. If we go far enough, we would reach a place with tundra and without trains. You could learn to drive a bulldozer. I could dictate. At the end of the day, you'd be too tired to communicate. Do you know that in some countries the workday is sixteen hours long and there is no lunch, air conditioning, or ergonomic chairs?"

"Is this supposed to make me feel better?"

"No, it's supposed to make you feel worse."

I knew what the dictator was saying—perspective. People drown all the time, some in oceans and others in bowls of chicken soup. I should have had perspective the day Todd had bolted out of Café Fortuna after he had finished his second beer and I'd walked into an emptied apartment. He had packed all his things while I was at work, including the tent we bought together for camping and the snowboard I had given him for his birthday, and loaded it all into his car. That explained the single Ha. His hands had been busy, packing.

My father called yesterday and asked how Todd was. I hadn't told him that Todd had left. My father cannot live my happy life for me if he knows I'm not happy. I promised to visit him next week; he complained about pains in his lower back, which he usually did when he ran out of money.

The dictator asked if I could build him a mausoleum, preferably two mausoleums: one to house his body and the other for the body of his double. Nothing too extravagant, he said, but it should have a perfectly square footprint. The second mausoleum, the one for the body double, should be a mirror image of the first, but an inch smaller in every measurement—he wouldn't want the body double to develop an overinflated ego.

"But you don't even have a double," I said.

"That's your problem," he said. "You choose to focus on limitations, your own and others'. At least after my death those who came to worship me would have options."

Lately, he has been spending a lot of time polishing the walls of the jar. He would moisten his fingers with saliva, rub and rub, and step back to examine his reflection. He would tilt his head, turn sideways, and puff his cheeks. Then he would give me a look of quiet resentment.

"You haven't noticed," he said.

"What?"

He pointed to his cheeks. I leaned in closer and saw a few stubbly greyish hairs.

"How?" I asked.

"Clap," he said.

"Turritopis dohrnii is a bell-shaped species of medusa, measuring a maximum of 0.2 inches in diameter. An adult has about eighty tentacles. The stomach is crimson red and the jelly in the walls of the bell is uniformly thin. The jellyfish can be found in the Mediterranean Sea and in the waters of Japan. The unique feature exhibited by this species is a certain form of immortality. It is the only known case of an animal capable of

reverting back to the stage of sexual immaturity after having reached the stage of sexual maturity."

"No kidding," I said.

"You cannot interrupt a dictation! You're not the dictator, I am."

He looked like he was about to burst into tears.

"I'm sorry," I said. "This is unbelievable."

"For those who cannot think outside the box," he snapped.

I let that one go. I noticed that he had developed a twitch in his left eye and I wasn't sure if it was the stress or the caffeine.

"In the early 1980s, scientists began to harvest the medusa cells while they were in their transitional stage. They tested them to see if they could cure hormonal imbalances or be used as a night cream or nutritional supplements. Unfortunately, the cells proved to be neither harmful nor beneficial. The research was abandoned. One day, an eight-year-old girl found a Ziploc bag with ashy powder in a drawer during a Take Your Daughter to Work Day. She mixed it with water and built a tiny snowman. Imagine everyone's shock when the next day it began to walk, talk, and claim to be a building inspector."

He got up to signal the end of the dictation. "The dictators are rare," he said, "especially since no one harvests the medusa cells anymore. A few of us were packaged and are still sold in souvenir shops. But, most likely, you would end up with a building inspector, a tax collector, or a furniture store manager. You were very lucky."

"Yes," I said. "I'm in my kitchen with a sexually immature and potentially immortal three-inch dictator. It's like falling into a sewer manhole and being thankful for not feeling the rain outside. How long can you keep on reverting?"

He pouted. "Statistically speaking, forever. But there are risks. There have been executions by flushing."

Thirty years from now, the dictator could still be in my kitchen, swinging between pre- and post-pubescence. Todd would grow bald and soft. The two yappy Maltese, the ones that leave puddles by the mailboxes, would be gone, along with their owner. In stormy weather, my bones would ache. I would grow calm—agitation feeds on hope, but how long can hope revert?

"What about the beard?" I changed the subject.

"I was hesitant to return back to puberty, but I believe in taking chances. If you had transitional cells, you'd agree." He gave me a condescending look. "While you were binge watching one of your series, I returned to sexual immaturity. I entered puberty about a quarter to four and stubble started coming through. In a few days, I will look like a Charles Darwin's body double."

The next morning, I saw that he dug up trenches in the clotted cream, which by now had hardened and looked like a dried up river bed. He was lying down in a trench, face down, and covered his ears when I clapped to switch him to *think big* mode. When I asked if he still thought about unicycles, he leapt to his feet, stepped back, and the heel of his boot got caught in the cream crevice. He fought to stay up, waving his arms as if his had eighty tentacles. But he fell on his behind with a sloppy thump and both of his guns fell out of their holsters.

This was not the best time to tell him that I was going to spend the weekend in Pennsylvania with my father. His face turned a newborn baby red and sorrowful. I would be back Sunday night, I pleaded, no later than seven, don't be a grouch. Don't be late, he countered.

"Must be nice," he added, "not to be confined to a jar."

Todd used to say that the walls of my apartment were stifling him, repressing his creative vision. I would try to lure him out for a jog. He would become all flustered and tell me my solutions were one-dimensional. But the dictator was smaller than Todd. On the way home from work, I stopped by a pet store and bought a fish tank. After a second thought I bought a plastic pearly castle and a wheel, the kind Benny had had. Benny would run and run on that thing until he fell off.

When I came home, the dictator was asleep. I'd never seen him sleep before. He was curled up, tight fists raised, as if he was trying to keep his dreams from escaping through his mouth. The fish tank made a clank when I put it down on the kitchen table. He stirred and opened his eyes.

"What's this?" he asked.

"It's the best I can do in a mausoleum-less situation."

He put an index finger to his temple, gesturing *shoot me*, told me that he'd never been so insulted and that in some countries I would be executed or exiled. I told him that he was the one complaining about cramped quarters and I would exile myself to Pennsylvania, but only for the weekend. He was lonely, I said, my father.

"Loneliness," the dictator said, "is a preconditioned response of a perpetually immature nervous system." Then he asked if he could come.

"Next time," I lied. My father was not unconventional enough for this visitor.

I brought Todd to Pennsylvania with me once, about a year into our relationship. Inside the old, flat, ranch-style house Todd looked deflated, like a kite that crashed into an electrical line.

Todd must be flying plenty of kites now, at the beach, in the Maldives, with Sasha. That's where they were going to live for a few months to concentrate on their art, he had told me before he split.

"We shouldn't be tied to a place," he said. "We shouldn't be following the maps our parents made; we should be making our own. We can reshape the space around us. Did you know that Alaska is three times the size of Texas?"

For two months before he left, each week, Todd would place an apple on my kitchen table. He would set up his flash and his camera and wait, wait to capture, he said, the interim moment of decomposition, when the apple would no longer be apple but not yet become compost. It was an emotionally taxing project, he said. He needed to recharge. He asked me to go away for a few months, to live off the grid or at least in San Francisco. I told him that if I left my job, my father would lose his house.

"Your father is an adult," Todd said. "He should be responsible for his own financial situation."

I knew that he should be, but he wouldn't be. Two years back, he quit his contracting job and began collecting miniature replicas of vintage cars. I would ask him about the mortgage or the bills and he would say that he couldn't be bothered. He had wasted enough time being mature, he said, worrying about mortgages, school districts, termites, and car insurance. He would rather worry about finding the replacement tires for his 1955 Porsche model. Solving smaller problems had bigger payoffs.

Todd had told me that I was not being supportive. Of

his art. Perhaps apples rot differently in the Maldives. Maybe, they, Sasha and Todd, would go for a swim one day and be eaten by carnivorous sea sponge. There are at least seven species of those known to scientists, the dictator had told me. Their bones, naked and polished, would wash ashore many months later.

"Are these the remains of prehistoric people?" a uniformed policeman would ask.

"No," a detective in a tropical shirt would reply, "these are bones of two classic modern assholes."

Friday morning I left for work with my overnight bag.

"I will be back on Sunday," I told the dictator. "I am sorry about the fish tank and the wheel. I bought you fresh roasted organic coffee beans."

"The castle could work as a mausoleum," he said. "It could be adequate, maybe if it had a balustrade or a tribune. A trapdoor in the floor would be nice with a small prison in the basement, nothing too lavish."

"We can talk about it when I come back," I said and poured a double dose of beans into the jar.

"Stay," he said. "I could move into the fish tank tonight and tell you about manatees."

"Sounds like a plan," I said. "Sunday night when I come back from my father's."

It's an indulgence to be the one who is leaving, like naps, cashmere socks, or pie a la mode.

I checked the weather for the weekend. Vicious, the forecast said, wind gusts and torrential downpours. I drew back the curtains, opened the kitchen window and moved the jar to the windowsill. The rain was clearing its throat with a drizzle and a few fat drops fell into the jar.

The dictator shivered and, with his back to me, asked me to close the window.

I told him humidity improves facial hair growth. He turned around. Tiny terrors written on tiny faces could be quite convincing. But I walked out the door before I could decide what my intentions were.

I didn't tell him that I knew a thing or two about manatees—aside from the time they raise their young, manatees are solitary animals and spend half of their lives underwater. Manatees are unique because they only have six vertical vertebrae. All other mammals have seven. But manatees do well managing with less, without things they don't know they need.

I called my father to confirm I was coming. He picked up after a half a ring, his voice, sleepy at first, turned into a bouncy ball. He asked me if I was bringing Todd.

"We broke up," I said.

"I'm so sorry, honey." His voice got quiet.

"Don't be. I'm not."

Over three Todd-less months had passed. If I could, for a moment, revert to the time when we were sitting at Café Fortuna, I still wouldn't cry. No, I would cry. Then I would tell Todd that deep at the very bottom of that mud puddle he calls his soul, where no amoeba, or medusa, let alone a manatee, would ever live, I knew what he knew, that he made his photographs black and white because they were not very good. It takes guts to take pictures in color; he was too afraid to be called an amateur. Then I would still tell him to eat Black Valor's shit.

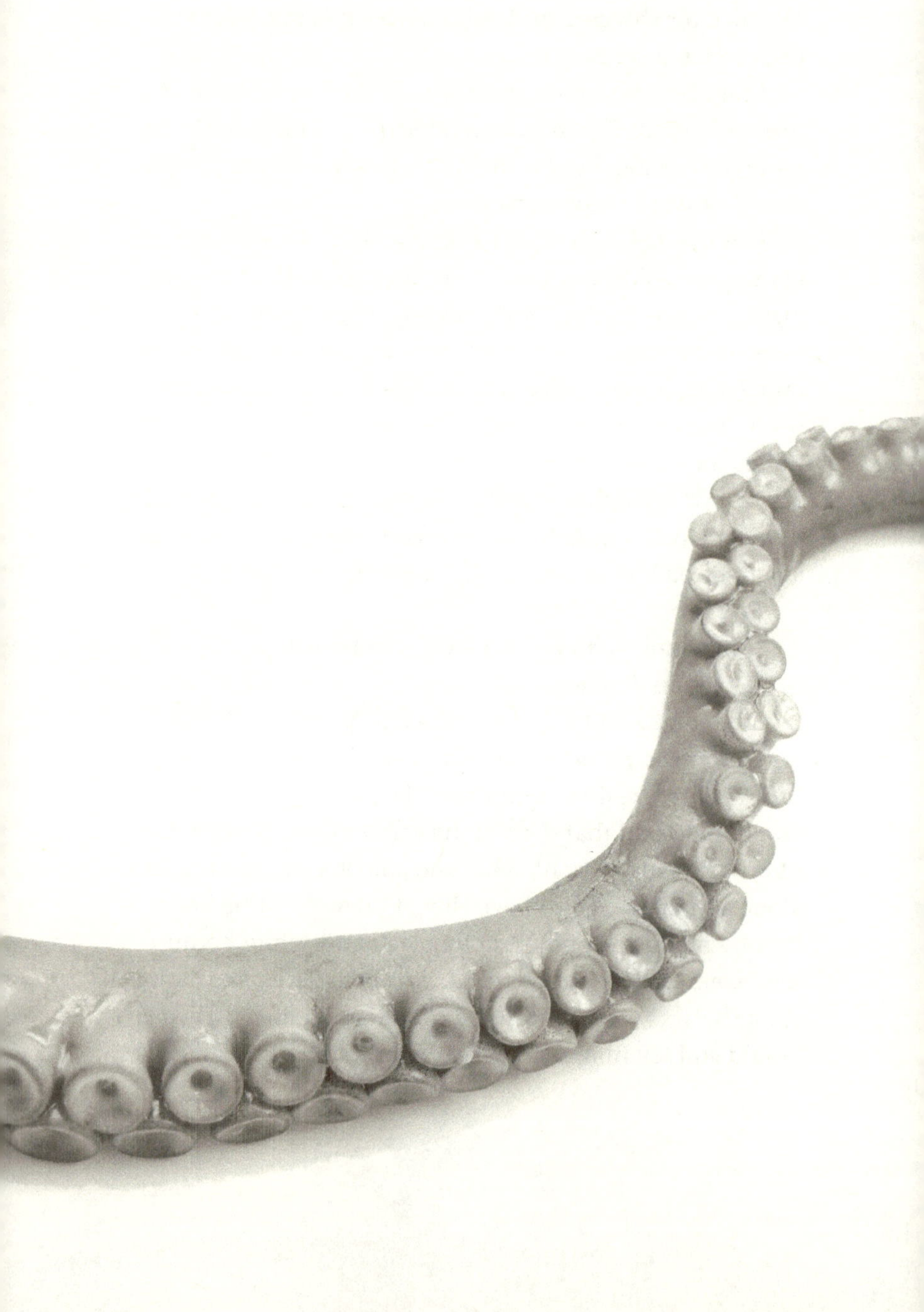

CHIROPTERA

Kayla Pongrac

CHIROPTERA

Kayla Pongrac

They say that when bats exit caves, they always turn left.
If I were a bat, I wouldn't leave my cave; I would remain
upside-down in my dark corner, embracing the pulsing
echolocation, swaddling each message underneath my
thin wings, which refused me flight, per my request. At
night I would invite the moths and mosquitoes into my
mouth and let them linger briefly on the bristles of my
tongue, where they could feel the heat of my language
and appreciate the thrill of acknowledging only one
possible direction.

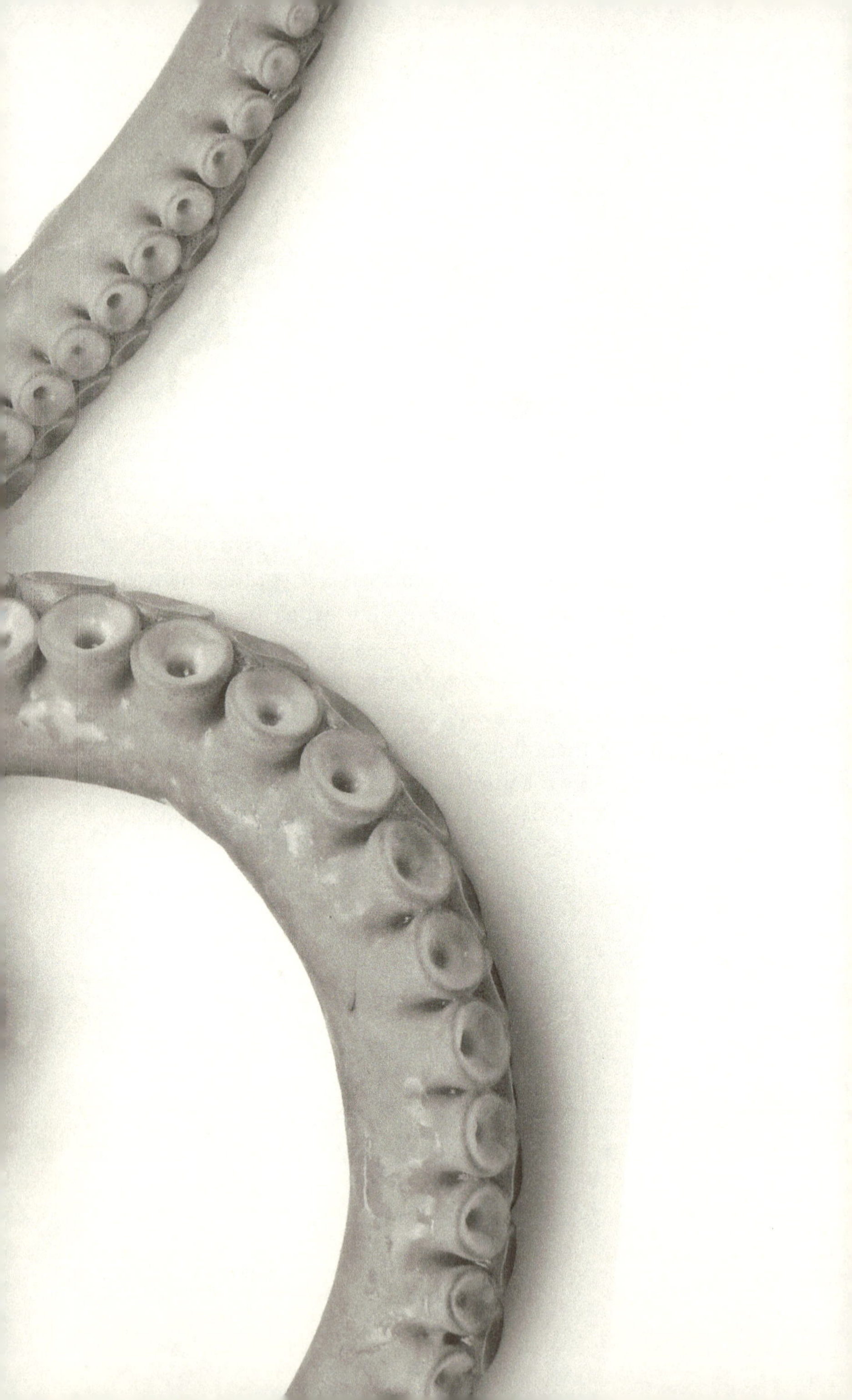

SHAMPOO

Ingrid Jendrzejewski

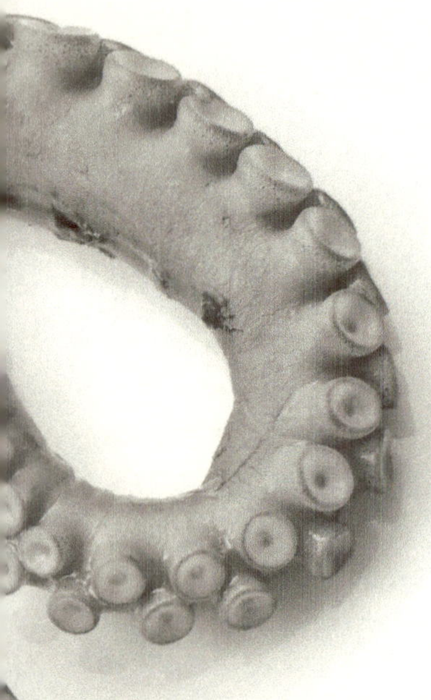

SHAMPOO

Ingrid Jendrzejewski

On numerous occasions, I've wished that I were not a husband at all, but in fact, a bottle of my wife's shampoo. There is something about being scrubbed on somebody's scalp that evokes an intimacy that is beyond what could ever be achieved in our bedroom. To be squeezed out daily, cupped in her hand, melted into the creases of her palm and the whorls of her fingertips; to cherish, up close, skin un-blanched by eyes or sun, the grey shafts not yet touched by dye; to be frothed into madness by scrambling fingers, so close to that trembling, unfathomable mind that lies beneath her scalp: this is what I long for.

But then, a bottle of shampoo is so finite. The contents are used up quickly, the empty bottle discarded without a thought. A day or two after a shower, natural oils creep back into the hair, matting it, greasing it, erasing the memory of the perfect clean, that act of transcendent communion that occurs when the surface tension between water and soil is reduced.

Perhaps, though, that ephemeral relationship is what I long for most. Perhaps I could know her better if, when in my presence, she didn't consider me. Perhaps we could finally come to some sort of understanding if she, stripped of all clothing and pretensions, simply used me for quiet purposes, sucking me dry and then throwing me into the rubbish, where I would have to face the delightful debaucheries of decomposition and decay with only the memory of her fingerprints on my hollow, plastic shell.

BUTTERBEAN

Emily Koon

BUTTERBEAN

Emily Koon

When the baby appeared on her mantel shelf, singing its heart out and kicking its legs, Pamela thought she was having one of her dreams.

The one where the baby comes out a full-grown adult and splits her body open.

The one where it's the consistency of gelatin, its insides visible. The red gummy heart beats bravely, the pink gummy lungs rising and falling, bringing Pamela in and out like the tides. The doctor says, "Nothing to worry about; he's just gummy."

But she did worry. Her dreams were always about that.

The child on her mantel shelf wasn't gummy or a dream. He looked like a carnival kewpie, with a lick of yellow hair on his head. Otherwise baldheaded. She called him Butterbean.

"Ooh wee oooh wee oh," Butterbean sang night and day. When his voice gave out, he whistled.

"Oh, Butterbean, you unexpected gift," Pamela said.

"Ooh ee oh ee oh woo," he sang for the joy of life, babbling in that weird alien language of children just learning to speak.

. . .

Before Butterbean became hers, Pamela tried to give him back. Return the gift.

"Babies don't just show up on people's mantels," said the police officer who took her call. She thought Pamela was a nutcase.

Pamela knew babies didn't just turn up like that, but this wasn't a hallucination, a fabrication of events. She explained how for ten years she'd had an important job doing public relations for Organic Aromatics, the country's number one maker of natural body products.

"Balms and whatnot, nothing with harsh chemicals."

The factory reminded her of Willy Wonka, with giant mixers turning twenty-four hours a day and people scurrying in white jumpsuits like Oompa Loompas, pouring oils and butters into the pots. Every now and then, someone found an Oompa Loompa toe in their hair wash, and she wrote press releases that made them forget. *The toe was reattached without loss of motor function.* There were a lot of accidents, lots of strange things happening among the vats, so she was busy. Her press releases were like magic spells. She worked her will on the will of others, shifting them into alternate dimensions where facts were different, making changes to the timeline.

Sometimes she thought of her own life in terms of a press release heading. *Local woman gets everything she ever wanted.* What she wrote had a way of coming to be.

The police officer transferred to her Behavioral Health. They told her the same thing: babies didn't appear out of thin air. Would she mind coming in for a psychiatric screening?

"I would mind that very much," she said and hung up the phone.

After that, Butterbean was hers. She rocked him in the silver light of late night television, before work, whenever he'd let her. Through David Letterman, Jon Stewart, Jerry Springer, the Home Shopping Network, reruns of *Mary Tyler Moore* and *The Gong Show*. He wouldn't be hers forever. He'd go off to college one day, join a fraternity, register with the Green Party. He might slip out of her hands and back into the fold in space he tumbled out of.

Butterbean went along with the rocking. He'd rather have been sitting on the mantel shelf, singing his nonsense, but having someone to love him wasn't bad. He hadn't come there to be her baby, but he understood that letting the woman rock him was a small price to pay for singing his song.

■　　■　　■

When she was a little girl, Pamela got one of those battery operated crawling dolls for Christmas. Its name was Baby Get Up and Go. She'd circled it in the Sears catalog, the only thing she wanted that year, but once she had it, it was kind of weird. It had that terrible tickle laugh all dolls had, like an unclean spirit had been imprisoned in its voice box. But unlike regular dolls, this one laughed for no reason, in the middle of the night, in rooms by itself. After that bad babysitter, Kirsten, let her watch *Chucky*, Pamela became sure it would come to life and attack her. She decided not to sit around waiting for the axe to drop. One day, she took Baby Get Up and Go out to the sidewalk and sent it waddling down the street, out of her life.

■　■　■

Pamela's downstairs neighbor Felix could see Butterbean too.

The night he found out about Butterbean, Felix dropped by her apartment, fancying a bite at the Persian place.

"Been thinking about kabobs all day," he said.

This was a lie. He was thinking about her, the night of that awful *Battlestar Galactica* marathon when she ripped his heart out. Until three months ago, they were a sort-of couple, occasionally going out to dinner and movies and once an interpretive dance performance. The dancers had been naked except for a layer of turquoise paint.

During the ill-fated marathon, Felix's idea, Pamela admitted to herself that he was nice but kind of a dork. She didn't feel bad. He'd find someone else, eventually. She only wished for a little more space, a city block at least, between her and Felix. He couldn't completely let the relationship go, which was why every day he found some small excuse to make contact with her. There were drop-ins, texts about kabobs, weather, anything he could string between them.

Now Felix had a big excuse, something real to string between them. He tied one end to himself and the other to her, like patio lights.

"If we could just figure out how Butterbean got here. That's the biggest mystery of all, his materialization," Felix said, materializing closer to Pamela on the sofa. "Poor thing. Does he understand what we say to him?"

Pamela didn't like talking about where Butterbean came from. She knew if you pulled long enough on a thread, it eventually led you back to its source. She didn't want to go asking questions that would unravel the whole thing. Birth mothers, missing persons. And anyone could see there was a metaphysical reason for Butterbean's presence. Like the police officer said, babies didn't just appear on mantels.

"Maybe I could talk to him in German," Felix said. His grandparents emigrated from Germany in the thirties, which was how he knew a little.

"I don't think the language is the issue. Butterbean is a baby."

Felix scooted closer and put his arms around her, smelling beefy like the kabobs he'd picked up. She felt hungry, but not for him.

"You're a baby. You're my baby," he said. His lips gathered into a kiss and came at her. They filled Pamela's apartment.

His hand went under the back of her shirt, going for her bra clasp, but before he could unhook it, Pamela remembered. Butterbean needed his bottle. It was an old trick from when they dated. He'd go at her bra and some urgent need would surface. The dishwasher needed starting; the kitchen floor had a scum on it that had to be dealt with right then. It worked like a charm. Felix dematerialized from her cushion.

Local woman extricates self from Felix Gruber.

In the six months since Butterbean appeared, Felix had floated a dozen wild theories about him. He checked him for a hidden battery pack, making sure he wasn't a lifelike toy. He made jokes about Butterbean being a baby Cylon. *There are many copies, and Butterbean has a plan.* Lately, the mystery was deepening. Butterbean wasn't growing like other babies. He should have been more than a year old, but he wasn't walking, putting little sentences together, anything.

Felix took Butterbean's lack of development into account.

"He must have a genetic disorder that's keeping him from aging on the traditional trajectory. It must be why his birth family rejected him."

"You think he's Benjamin Buttoning," Pamela said.

"It's the only thing that fits."

The fact that Butterbean could sit on the mantel shelf all day without falling off, even while Pamela was at work, seemed like proof of this. What real nine-month-old could you leave in the house alone all day, as Pamela did? What baby didn't grow, Felix insisted, if there wasn't a full-grown adult living inside it?

"That doesn't prove anything," Pamela said, thinking of the dream where her baby comes out a college student.

"I read an article this morning that said scientists figured out how to reverse the aging process in mice. They mucked around with the chromosomes. Elderly mice ended up with the bones and muscles and skin of newborns. Pamela, Butterbean could be a hundred years old."

Butterbean wasn't a lab experiment gone wrong, a cuddly Frankenstein with a lick of yellow hair. Experiments like what Felix was talking about always went haywire, Pamela knew.

"Didn't you read *Flowers for Algernon* in high school?" she called in from the kitchen, where she filled bottle after bottle with formula.

"That was a fiction, Pamela. This is real life," Felix said, sweeping her concerns away. "What if he's regressing slowly, and he keeps getting younger until he's just an egg?"

Until he didn't exist. Pamela thought of Butterbean growing smaller and smaller, one day a three-month-old, a newborn, finally reverting to a fetal state. He would curl into a bean befitting his name, arms and legs withdrawn into buds. Then a round mass of pearly cells vibrating with potential, then nothing. Felix kept talking about chromosomes, his voice high and strained, some panic in it. Pamela let the noise recede until Felix was a *rawr-rawr-rawr* at the edge of her hearing. Like a brown bear pawing its way into a beehive. *Let me in-let me in-let me in.*

. . .

When Pamela's sister was born, their parents named her Denise, but Pamela wanted to call her She-ra: Princess of Power. Like the doll from the Sears catalog, her sister came out different than she'd thought. Fragile and spastic, the skin on her eyelids and nostril arches almost see-through. A lace of fine veins ran under all her surfaces. Pamela thought if she stared at Denise long enough, she could see through her to the red gummy heart beating in her chest.

One day, she sneaked into the nursery and got Denise out of the crib. Pamela misjudged the baby's weight and fell backwards onto the carpet, clutching for dear life the weird little sister who'd thrown off the balance in the house. Her parents were like children themselves, doing things Pamela didn't understand. Buying a new car when the old one was fine. Did money grow on trees? She worried they didn't know what they were doing, bringing more kids into the world, and when their incompetence came to light, she'd have to take care of Denise.

Denise didn't hit her head or anything—nothing bad

happened, not now with Pamela holding her, not later in Denise's life that she could ever see—but she cried anyway.

"Shut up, Denise," Pamela said.

"Don't tell Denise to shut up," her father said as he and their mother ran in.

"And you shouldn't pick her up without help. Denise is not a doll," her mother said.

She had plenty of those in her room. The one from Sears must have been halfway to California by then. She wondered. If she put Denise out on the sidewalk, how far would she get?

▪ ▪ ▪

Christmas Day, Pamela's family tried to unspool the truth about Butterbean. They stared at him, then at Pamela, then back at Butterbean, as though the answers would be read in their skins. When this failed, the questions. How long was the foster arrangement for, was there hope of adoption? Was there a man back in the city, someone with a lick of yellow hair?

"The social worker's name was Deb," Pamela said to sidetrack them. "She had a Midwest accent, maybe Minnesota."

"All right, we believe you," her mother said.

"Why foster parenting, exactly, is what I want to know," Denise said.

Denise and her husband Arthur had five little stair-steppers, identical blonde children that budded off Denise once a year like sea sponges. Arthur made good money in the electronics industry, enough for their Tudor Revival, for all those children, for Denise to not work and to go around in skinny pants made of shimmery material. Her holiday pants.

"I wanted to help. The social worker was very persuasive," Pamela said.

A credible answer would have been, *All of a sudden, I felt an emptiness in my life.* Denise would have seen a crevasse open up inside Pamela, a long stretch of quiet years passing. She'd have felt embarrassed at her life's riches and let it go.

Pamela didn't mention Felix.

Before the holiday there was a fight. He knew it didn't make them a real family—he kept saying this, that he understood how things were—but he wanted to spend the holiday with her and Butterbean. He wanted to see Butterbean's face on Christmas morning, those mounds of presents he'd bought for them arranged under Pamela's tree. It was heartless, she knew, but if she wasn't careful, Felix would insinuate himself further into her life, into the apartment. He'd started bringing little gifts for Butterbean, dropping by to ask if she needed anything, then sticking around until all hours. He'd be living with them by Easter.

Felix's voice reached a squeaking pitch as he pleaded with her. Pamela heard herself saying she was going to her parents' for the holiday, even though she hadn't planned to. Now here she was, confusing her family by showing up with a baby. Confusing them by showing up at all. Felix saw through her. In the six years she'd lived in the apartment above his, he never once remembered her going anywhere for the holidays. This was why he'd said that thing about her, the awfulness she couldn't forgive.

You're the one regressing, Pamela. Curling up into yourself. You'll curl up so far there won't be room for anyone else. One day, you'll curl up so far your atoms will fuse and there won't be anything left. You'll curl so far up they'll put up a sign that will read, "Here is a person who used to exist. Here is a person who shut out the world."

That evening, after the gifts were exchanged, Pamela and her mother took Butterbean upstairs and put him in the crib, which had been Pamela's once.

"Oh-wee-ohh-wee-oh," sang Butterbean. He kicked his legs just like he did on the woman's mantel shelf, wondering why he couldn't sit on the one here. It was a perfectly good shelf. It was in the room with all the presents, but the room was now an impassible ocean of ribbon and tissue paper. There was an ocean where he was before. It surrounded everything and he couldn't cross it because of the things in it. That must have been why.

"Hush singing now, Butterbean," Pamela's mother said.

The singing stopped, and he grabbed his feet, thinking what it meant to have a grandmother, a place to spend summer holidays. To have an aunt, cousins, people with shared histories but who'd come out *different*. He kicked his legs happily at the thought of family pictures and Easter egg hunts.

When he'd settled down, Pamela's mother curled his hair lick around her finger.

"I've been trying to figure out who Butterbean reminds me of," she said. "It's that awful doll you had, the one that laughed like a demon."

"That horrible thing," Pamela said.

"I never knew why you wanted it. It was just lifelike enough to be disturbing. But it had a little skootch of yellow hair over its forehead, just like Butterbean. Wonder what happened to it?"

Local woman's windup doll circles globe, returns home decades later. Thirty years was enough time for anything to come full circle.

.   .   .

In her twenties, Pamela went on the pill, even though she wasn't having sex. It seemed smart and prepared, like life was a desert of shifting sands and she could be thrown onto a new track any minute. The nurse explained how things worked hormonally.

"All those eggs you were born with, they stay right up in their basket."

It made her feel like a hen. Every time she took her pill, she said, *cluck cluck cluck.*

About that same time, she started having the baby dreams. In the most common one, she was unemployed, facing eviction. Because she still wasn't having sex, she ran through the other possibilities:

1. Immaculate conception
2. Alien impregnation
3. Asexual reproduction, like a sea sponge, budding off itself

She lay in the bathtub pretending to be a sponge, her fibrous skeleton swaying in the current.

When the baby came out, it was a litter of kittens that went running off in every direction. As hard as she tried, she couldn't hold on to even one.

.   .   .

One day, Pamela came home from work, and Butterbean

wasn't there. Not on the mantel shelf, not anywhere.

"Butterbean, Butterbean?" she called into every room. In response, the echo of her own voice through the apartment

That Butterbean might disappear as suddenly, as mysteriously as he'd come had been somewhere in her thoughts all this time. Felix asked once what they'd do if that happened. Was there a missing children hotline for paranormal babies? Call the police, of course, what any parent would do. But she didn't. She knew Butterbean wasn't kidnapped or down a well like Baby Jessica. The fold in space had opened back up and he'd rolled into it. That was all. She sat down and listened to her empty apartment, to her life clicking along with the radiator. She curled into herself.

Local woman falls into the abyss.

A few months after Butterbean disappeared, the baby dreams started again. Pamela took a few weeks of personal leave and sat around the apartment watching *Kathie Lee & Hoda*, waiting for him to reappear. She ignored Felix's knocks at the door, his text pleas piercing her quiet. *I'm sorry for what I said. Is Butterbean ok? The Persian place has a new vegetarian kabob.*

Eventually, the knocks and texts stopped. Pamela started hearing voices through the bathroom vent. Felix met someone. She took to lying on the tile and listening to his dates, as they prepared endless food that popped and sizzled and reminded Pamela that she was alone, had endless arguments about which independent film directors were best. Often the theme music from *Battlestar Galactica* played in the background. She heard all the explosions when the Cylons caught up with the fleet.

"Where's your soy sauce? We can't eat this without soy

sauce. It'd be, like, a travesty," whoever the woman was said one night. The woman inserted *like* into her speech pauses so often Pamela had to put a pillow over the vent. She went back to watching *Frasier* reruns on Netflix.

Local woman hits bottom.

When Butterbean didn't rematerialize, Pamela fell back into a routine at Organic Aromatics. The space-time continuum, or whatever had ripped, repaired itself. The gears of her life started grinding again. She wrote press release after press release, had lunch in the employee cafeteria, a corporate suited person in a sea of Oompa Loompas. The Oompa Loompas only talked about work. How you had to get the pH right or people's hair would fall out. *Local woman succumbs to ennui.*

In the spring, a reporter asked to work on the bath bomb floor. He was doing an in-depth on the all-natural craze. He got high on the Epsom salts and menthol in the Creme de Mental mini-bombs, and Pamela had to cast a spell to keep it out of the paper. *Crème de Mental mini-bombs are made of carefully tested, all-natural ingredients you have in your kitchen pantry. If used as directed, they transport consumers to another world, a place of relaxation and well-being.* The reporter disappeared without a trace.

Pamela didn't go to work so much as it came to her. She began to wonder if the whole Butterbean thing had been one of her dreams after all, a past life thing, anything other than reality, rocking a flesh and blood baby while David Letterman's tooth gap filled the television screen.

Then, in June, an eyelid appeared in the foot salve, its long curling lash intact. *The owner appears to have been female,* she wrote. It made everything all right, because all the employees on the foot salve floor were male. No one came forward to claim the eyelid.

That night, Pamela gave birth to twins in a dream. The first baby was a standard baby, nothing gelatinous. She cradled it in her arms, terrified at the prospect of motherhood but relieved she was no longer alone.

"Not so fast," the doctor said when she asked when she could take the baby home. "There's one more coming out."

At first, she thought the second baby was a flounder—she'd dreamed of birthing fish before, pasty-white slabs of grouper and tilapia slithering onto the floor—but it was in fact a giant eyelid, its long, curling lash intact.

"Maybe someone mucked around with the chromosomes?" the doctor said.

The nurse cocked her head and smiled, hoping to be half this lucky someday. Maybe a toenail, a couple of teeth still embedded in a hunk of gum.

Pamela hugged the babies close, wanting to be alone with them, but the others in the room closed in on her. She didn't blame them. All they wanted was to share this moment, be there when the news crew arrived. Maybe they'd be quoted on the air, something about life rolling inexorably into the next generation, in spite of everything. In spite of toes in shampoo bottles and Cylons and what you had to leave behind for moments like this to exist. But, mostly, everybody wanted to see the eyelash. They all wanted a closer look at that.

THE EATING HABITS OF FAMOUS ACTORS

Zach Powers

THE EATING HABITS OF FAMOUS ACTORS

Zach Powers

All the main characters are dead now. I am afraid I'm all you have left. You probably noticed me in a couple of scenes. I was there. Less beautiful, scripted with less erudition, less suavity. My wardrobe was selected for neutrality, my lines written for the simple advancement of plot. I made no bold declarations, no professions of love. I delivered the facts so my more prominent, more romantic counterparts could voice lines as if reciting poetry. The soft focus of their faces filled the whole screen for every smile and tear, while I stood, smallish, in the perpetual background of my existence.

They're all gone now, as the real names of the people who pretended to be them scroll up the screen, accompanied by a swelling string orchestra (there goes the name of the man who pretended to be me). The copyright halts in the center of the screen and the music fades and then everything is black. This is usually when you leave, if not before. But we are still here now, together.

What is my name? Military Officer #2. On my costume, on an embroidered patch, chest-high, right, it says Pendleton. My rank insignia makes me a colonel. But in the script I am identified only as Military Officer #2. I am too young to be a colonel. I know this, and you, the observant viewer, must have noticed it. I have no obvious subordinates, partake of no battles, lack even a gun. But I am Military Officer #2. I will tell you my story.

There is an explosion, shown from many different angles so you can appreciate the pyrotechnics. I am with a group of people like me. Soldiers and Lab Techs and Townspeople. Lab Tech #1 and Military Officer #1 are shown in close-up, tears of admiration in their eyes (tears that net them considerably more pay than the rest of us). Then you are looking down from a helicopter. The view pulls farther out and the fire is a small, yellow speck on the landscape. An ocean creeps into view. It is supposedly the Pacific, but we filmed on the coast of Maine. The camera pans up until the screen is filled with sky. Fade to black. Credits.

We are on a vista, those of us still alive, overlooking the burning facility. This is the sort of location that you only ever see in movies. You've never experienced a vista from which you can watch important action. Important action happens where it will, with little regard for scenery.

The explosion wasn't that impressive to us. It won't realize its onscreen glory until the digital effects people get their hands on it. They will expand the ball of fire. They will add a shower of debris and plumes of smoke. Maybe even a mushroom cloud. Was there a mushroom cloud? I have no way of knowing until I sit beside you, watching myself watch the thing that wasn't actually there for me to watch.

One by one we walk away, leaving Lab Tech #1 and Military Officer #1 behind. Their close-up has separated them from the rest of us. One day you will see them in a different movie and wonder where you've seen them before. You will wonder for days. You will wake up in the middle of the night and remember. *The vista.* There were other people with them, but you remember only these two.

Townsperson #3 walks with her head tilted back, looking up at the forest canopy. She has known this forest for as long as she can remember, as long as she doesn't remember too far back. This whole Californian coastline is her home. These trees, the likes of which do not grow in California, are hers, as are the species of birds unique to the East Coast, and other animals, and the color of the ocean.

Behind us, the facility continues to burn, making loud cracks, sounds that will be replaced in the final version of the film with a steady roar. The cracking fades as we move farther away. You'd think we would be upset, but we knew all along the fate of the facility. It was there in the script. We knew the flames before we saw them.

I've forgotten how long the walk back to town is because we've been cutting from one place to another with impossible immediacy for the last two hours. Beads of sweat burst through the layer of makeup on our faces. Solider #5 wipes his forehead with his sleeve and smears flesh tone across the camouflage fabric. Two of the older Townspeople stop and rest on a rock. We leave them behind. The scene on the vista was their last.

The trees thin out and the low buildings of the town become visible. Once-white walls yellowed by time, small, square windows full of yellow light. Towns like this, lethargic and homey, are perfect counterpoints for the action of a movie like ours. Through convention, when seen on screen, instead of providing the comfort they would in reality, these towns instead inspire agitation.

You are conditioned to anticipate the shattering of the illusion of tranquility. Plus, you've seen the previews. Before you ever sat in your seat in the darkened theater you had seen the final explosion, from at least two of its dozen angles, many times on TV. The last time you came to the movies, prior to the movie you had come to see, you were treated to three minutes of this town overrun with gunfights and car chases. You've seen beneath the surface. But it is a real town, not a set, and outside the realm of our movie, it is, in fact, peaceful. With the main characters dead and burned up and resting comfortably in their trailers, there is nothing to upset the image of this town. It is what it looks like. You may abandon your previous apprehension. If this weakens the plot of the story I'm telling now, then so be it. I will lie about this town no longer.

The streets are empty except for those of us returning from the vista. The crew has already packed up all the equipment and rolled out in the trucks. The extras have gone back home. Most were from neighboring towns. They are left unmentioned in the credits. They sat next to you in the theater and waited for themselves to appear on screen, pointing out stray limbs in the tangle of crowd shots, claiming ownership of this hand or that elbow. You shushed one of them.

The actual townspeople, as opposed to our Townspeople, are all at home eating dinner by now. At first they were excited when the film crews arrived. They stood behind tapelines and watched as famous people said things to other famous people. But after weeks and weeks of disrupted lives, I know they will be glad to see us go.

I tell Solider #2 to get me a cup of coffee. It is the last

time I will have this authority. I will remove the uniform and everyone will remember that I was never a solider, much less an officer. I sit on a bench in the town square. The square is a small, grassy spot where they planted trees instead of built buildings. The grass around the base of the bench has grown taller than the top of my boots. Lab Tech #7 sits next to me, but we do not speak. We have no lines to say to each other. Soldier #2 never returns with my coffee.

Several Townspeople claim the gazebo in the middle of the square. They are talking and laughing and sharing stories like old friends. They have known each other for years, though we all met only a couple of months ago, and they have just together experienced the kind of adventure that doesn't usually happen to Townspeople. The first round of laughter is over and they realize that they have no other history, nothing much before the vista. They get up, patting shoulders and shaking hands. They walk each in a different direction, as if they were the debris expelled in an explosion.

Lab Tech #7 rises from the bench and walks off, her white lab coat billowing ghostlike behind her. I want to say goodbye, but I am unsure of exactly how I should say it. I am unsure of *who* is saying it. My uniform feels suddenly uncomfortable.

There are only three of us left in the square. Soldier #3 and Angry Townsperson hold hands on the other side of the gazebo. I see them as black shapes against the sunset. The clouds are distant and flat and gray. The trees barely have any green left in them. It is a beautiful scene but maybe too obvious. It announces the end too loudly.

We all, the men at least, tried to woo Soldier #3 from the first day of filming. I did my charming best over the cold cuts on the catering table to impress her. But there was Angry Townsperson. You recognize him from a TV show. He was younger then, just a kid, but you remember the cut of his jaw, and now he has the broad shoulders to match. When he doesn't shave at least twice a day, a thick growth of stubble covers his cheeks.

The sun is gone over the horizon. The shadows kick up like dust. I watch the couple leave the square, still holding hands, and for a moment, I forget their names. Jen and Ryan? No, that's not right. She is just a Soldier. He is a Townsperson, albeit an Angry one. I am a Military Officer.

The lamps flicker on in the empty park. I look down at my chest to remember my name, but I can't read the patch in the low light. The streets are still empty. People don't wander the streets at night in small towns. Nightlife is a phenomenon of the big city. I used to have a life there, in the city, before boot camp, before casting. It is a place that I would never have walked alone.

I round the corner and the darkness is overcome by the glow of a movie theater marquee. In mixed black and red letters it says the name of our movie. I fish money from one of the many pockets of my uniform and I buy a ticket. Inside, a zit-faced boy takes my ticket and salutes me. It seems like I have not seen a zit in forever. I salute back. It is an unfamiliar gesture. I am the highest-ranking officer in the movie and have been, until now, on the receiving end of all salutes. My fingertips touch my eyebrow and it is unclear which part of me is feeling the other.

The theater is dark. I follow the little lights in the floor and ascend the steps. I move into the row. I sit down next to you. Now you are part of the story. You were the audience, now you are The Audience. There is no one else in the theater. It is too dark to see your face. We'll call you #1. Audience Member #1. Don't say anything until you're supposed to. And never, ever look at the camera.

APPLES

Theodora Ziolkowski

APPLES

Theodora Ziolkowski

Digging is what I do when Stepmother is so angry that she sleeps the day away. I like the sight of the bearded roots and clearish gold slugs clinging to the end of my shovel, the feel of cracking into the ground in search of nothing in particular.

You can find so many things in an apple orchard. And that is where I am when I find the buried case.

Upstairs in the safe and sound of my room, I open it. Inside are bottles all tinted amber and miniature like toys, and each of these bottles is filled with a blood-red dye. Sometimes a vendor carrying a similar case comes knocking on the door to speak to Stepmother. "Cosmetics, would you like to buy some cosmetics?" she asks. Every time, Stepmother tries all the vendor's lipsticks, blushers, and powders, listening intently as the vendor, with her pointy black shoes, holds a mirror in front of Stepmother's face, tells her what is what. Afterward, the vendor stays for apple bread, applesauce, apple butter. Then she leaves with a basket of our apples, Stepmother goes to bed still wearing her makeup, and everyone gets what everyone wanted.

I take off my eye patch and burrow my fingernails

into my puffy lid, trying to make a scenario for the buried case, thinking maybe the bottles are for Big Sister, who uses the red to paint the dolls in her dioramas. Or maybe the bottles are for Stepmother, who is trying to make her hair look wild and young like Big Sister's.

I return the bottles, close the case, and tuck it under my bed when I hear Stepmother up from her snooze. She is slamming dishes around, probably getting ready to bake bread, which is what she does when she is not staring at the face that stares back at her in her mirrors.

"Ahem, ahem."

Big Sister is in the doorway.

She stuffs her hands in her pockets, asks how I am, and I say, "I am fine, how are you?" And Big Sister says that she is fine too.

"Put your patch back on," she says gently. "Oh, please stop rubbing, or like Stepmother says, you'll ruin your skin."

Later that night, we find Stepmother standing over the stove. She is wearing a big, floppy rag to hide her gray curls.

She divides her apple bread into three big chunks and doesn't look at us.

Big Sister and I thank Stepmother. We eat.

■　■　■

Fall arrives, and the vendor visits more often.

She takes kindly to Big Sister, asks if she would like a touch-up here or there as she holds up her blusher and brush.

She begins to bring Big Sister presents. Things like a small statue of an ebony cat, even a silk sash to accessorize a dress.

Shortly after she gives Big Sister a gemstone comb, Stepmother takes to breaking things: picture frames, vases, and clocks; the teapot and bread pans; the cobalt blue planters. From the doorway, I watch her lift the cookie jar shaped like a beehive and smash it to the floor.

The morning Stepmother finds her first wrinkle she covers every mirror in our house with a sheet.

There is nothing left to eat in the pantry but apples.

The vendor does not come the next day or the day after that.

■　■　■

The apple orchard is furred in frost when the dolls from Big Sister's dioramas disappear. And even though Big Sister continues to look everywhere, in all the drawers and shelves, even under the bed pillows, her dolls are nowhere to be found.

At the edge of the forest, I find a pair of pointy black shoes, an empty basket, and a broom.

■　■　■

Apples drop from the trees like shriveled fists.

I am pulling the last good apples from the branches when I notice the mound of dirt between two of the trees. Beside it is my shovel.

I give a soft kick to the lump of loam, crouch down,

and uncover a doll with a very pale face.

It must be one of Big Sister's!

The doll's bathrobe is grimy and her mouth is downturned. A spider scuttles across her tangled silver hair.

I ask Stepmother if I can clean the doll up and give it back to Big Sister, but Stepmother snatches the doll and says no, it is dirty, and all dirty things must go back in the ground where they belong.

She takes back the doll and grins at the spider.

"Stop itching," she scolds, swatting my hand from my patch.

.   .   .

Winter, the ground is white and glowing. Big Sister gets sick and Stepmother releases her curls from her rag.

I go to Big Sister's room with a tray of hot soup, but she is neither there nor in the attic or parlor. As far as I can tell, she is nowhere to be found.

I leave her lunch in the kitchen, put on my coat, and find her on the porch, curled up in the swing. Her face is so pale it's translucent; her hair is no longer red like the dye in the bottles, but the color of age and illness.

She tells me we need more apples. "For Stepmother," she explains as she stands and floats up to her room.

Stepmother eats the last of the good apples.

Big Sister won't stop touching my eye patch.

.   .   .

Come spring, Stepmother is still wearing her makeup and baking her bread. Stepmother is awake all day long but Big Sister is no more.

All of the sheets come off the mirrors.

Every night I take the case out from under my bed, touch all the bottles, and then put them back.

. . .

The day the ground is soft enough to begin digging again, I discover a second doll in the orchard. Specks of leaves stick to its crinkled face and its dove-white hair.

Drawing the doll up close, I notice one of its eyes is missing. Where there should be an eye is the smallest black pin.

When I try to remove it, my bad eye prickles. Once it is out, the doll's face smooths, and its lips turn rouge. Its hair lengthens, darkens into the color of crows.

I take off my patch and turn my face to the forest. Through my bad eye, I see the hills covered with the whitest snow and birds that prick the sky like cutouts of black paper. My hair feels fuller and hangs darker and heavier at my shoulders. The shaking hand clutching my eye patch is so white that for a moment I imagine myself suffocating in snow.

Back in my room, I fashion a tiny hand mirror from foil and a glass button. I find my favorite of Big Sister's dioramas and lay the doll down in one of its beds.

When I was a little girl and always trying to hide my eye patch, Stepmother used to tell me I was lucky I had at least one good eye: "One is enough to get by," she'd explain. Or, "Beauty for little girls isn't everything, you know. Beauty doesn't count quite yet. Just wait until you're older. Just wait until you'd do anything to get it back."

I tuck the doll under her quilt, scan the row of beds in her cozy new room, and count seven. I set the hand mirror in her hand—all the better to see herself.

[contributor bios]

Rita Bullwinkel lives in Nashville, Tennessee where she is a fiction MFA candidate at Vanderbilt University. Her writing has appeared in many places including *NOON, Spork, Joyland, The Atlas Review, Paper Darts*, and the book *Gigantic Worlds: An Anthology of Science Flash Fiction*. She is a graduate of Brown University, a Vanderbilt Commons Writer in Residence, a Sewanee Writers' Conference Tennessee Williams Scholarship Award winner, and a Helene Wurlitzer Foundation grantee. Read more about her at ritabullwinkel.com.

Ingrid Jendrzejewski studied creative writing and English literature at the University of Evansville before going on to study physics at the University of Cambridge. She has soft spots for go, cryptic crosswords, and the python programming language, but these days spends most of her time trying to keep up with a delightfully energetic toddler. Once in a very great while, she adds a tiny something to www.ingridj.com and tweets at @ LunchOnTuesday.

Emily Koon is a fiction writer from North Carolina. She has work in *Portland Review, Bayou, Atticus Review*, and other places and can be found at twitter.com/thebookdress.

[contributor bios]

Marina Petrova lives and writes in New York City. Her work has appeared in *The Brooklyn Rail, The Los Angeles Review of Books, Underwater New York*, and *Calliope Anthology*. She received an MFA from The New School in May 2014.

Kayla Pongrac is an avid writer, reader, tea drinker, and record spinner. She is also the founder of the artist collective A Permanent Income (apermanentincome. weebly.com). Kayla's first chapbook, a collection of flash fiction stories titled *The Flexible Truth*, is available for purchase from Anchor and Plume. Another chapbook, *Kettle Whistles the Blues*, is forthcoming in 2016 by Robocup Press. To read more of her work, visit kaylapongrac.com or follow her on Twitter @KP_the_Promisee.

Zach Powers lives and writes in Savannah, Georgia. His debut book, *Gravity Changes*, will be published in spring 2017 by BOA Editions. His work has appeared or is forthcoming in *Black Warrior Review, The Brooklyn Review, Forklift, Ohio, Phoebe, PANK, Caketrain*, and elsewhere. He is the founder of the literary arts nonprofit Seersucker Live (SeersuckerLive.com). He leads the writers' workshop at the Flannery O'Connor Childhood Home, where he also serves on the board of directors. His writing for television won an Emmy. Get to know him at ZachPowers.com.

[contributor bios]

Tamara K. Walker dreams of irrealities among typewriter ribbons, stuffed animals and duct tape flower barrettes. She resides near Boulder, Colorado with her wife/life partner and blogs irregularly about writing and literature at http://tamarakwalker.wordpress.com. She may also be found online at http://about.me/tamara.kwalker. Her writing has previously appeared or is forthcoming in *The Cafe Irreal*, *A cappella Zoo*, *Melusine*, *Apocrypha and Abstractions*, *Gay Flash Fiction*, *Identity Theory*, a handful of poetry zines, and several themed print anthologies published by Kind of a Hurricane Press.

Theodora Ziolkowski's poetry and prose have previously appeared or are forthcoming in *Glimmer Train*, *Prairie Schooner*, and *Short FICTION* (England), among other journals, anthologies, and exhibits. A chapbook of her poems, *A Place Made Red*, was published this year by Finishing Line Press. She is originally from Easton, Pennsylvania and currently lives in Tuscaloosa, Alabama.